# Native American Tales Retold

By Virginia Hawk Woman Smith and Wayne Gray Owl Appleton
Illustrated by Suzan A.M. McVicker

How Possum Got His Ugly Tail
retold by
Gray Owl

This story was printed in the Cherokee language in Indian
Territory in 1840. A version is included in Mooney's Myths of the
Cherokees. This is the first story I remember being told as a young
child.

A long time ago, the old people tell us that before the human beings came, all of the animals lived in towns and villages and they all spoke the same language.

One day the Chief of a large village decided to have a feast to celebrate the fine year and the harvest so he sent Rabbit—who was his messenger—to go to each animal and invite them to the feast in three days.

Every thing was going well until Rabbit got to Possum's house. In the old days, Possum didn't look like he does today. He still had a long nose and gray fur but he had the most beautiful furry tail—not the long skinny tail he has today. Possum was so proud of his beautiful tail—in fact he was vain about it. He thought he had the most beautiful tail of any of the animals.

"Hey Possum, Chief Bear is going to have a feast in three days—Are you going to come?"

Possum replied, "Of course I'm going to come—the only reason the other animals will be there is to see by beautiful tail. I wouldn't want to disappoint them".

Now Rabbit is a trickster and a joke-maker and this was just too much for him. He knew he needed to take Possum's vanity down a little.

Rabbit stepped back and admired Possum's tail. "You know, you are right! It is such a beautiful tail! I have an idea—let me get Grasshopper- our village barber- to come to your house on the morning of the feast to groom your tail. And I have a beautiful red ribbon that would go perfect on your tail. This will be my gift to the other animals".

Possum thought for a second and said, "You're right. That would be a lovely present for the village".

So Rabbit went on his way and made his arrangements but they weren't exactly what Possum thought because on the morning of the feast Grasshopper came to work on Possum's tail but instead of combing and brushing and fluffing the tail, he used the saw he has on the back of his leg to cut off every single hair right at the base. Then he used the red ribbon to hold all the hair in place and at the end of Possum's tail he tied a big red bow.

Possum looked at himself in the mirror and he was so proud—He was BEAUTIFUL. He spent the whole day admiring himself in the mirror and imagining how impressed the other animals would be by his beauty that night.

Finally, it came time for the feast and the dancing began. During the very first dance, Rabbit came close to Possum and reached out –and pulled loose the bright red bow. The ribbon began to unwind and – of course- since the ribbon was all that was holding the hair in place, the hair began to fall on the ground! Pretty soon all of the other animals could see what was happening and they made room for Possum to dance alone by himself in the Circle. Possum was so Proud—and so VAIN. Finally, just as the last of the ribbon came loose and the last hair fell to the ground, the other animals couldn't take it any more and they started to laugh.

"Why are they laughing?" Possum wondered—and then he saw the red ribbon on the ground and all of the hair. And when he looked back—instead of his beautiful wonderful tail—there was a long skinny thing that looked like a snake. Possum was horrified and so embarrassed! He didn't know what to do! Finally, he did the only thing he could think of and lay down and pretended that he was dead—hoping that the other animals would carry him out so he could sneak away. Which they did.

The old people told us that there are two things that are true to this day. One is that Creator left Possum with that ugly tail to remind him and the other animals not to be too Proud and Vain. The other thing is that whenever you see Possum in the woods or along the side of the road—if you shine a light on him he will lie down and pretend he is dead—because he knows that you are laughing at his ugly tail!

## How Rabbit Stole Otter's Coat
### retold by
### Gray Owl

A long time ago, the old people tell us that the world was a very different place and before the human beings came all of the animals lived together in towns and villages and they all spoke the same language.

One day on a fine late Fall afternoon, Chief Bear decided that he should have a Feast before all of the animals went their own ways for the Winter. So he sent his messenger Rabbit to each of the homes to invite all of the animals to come for a Feast in three days.

But as Rabbit went from home to home he got sadder and sadder.

When he looked at Fox he saw Fox's lovely tail and when he looked back at his own tail all he saw was that little cotton thing-and he was sad.

When he got to Raccoon's house he realized that Raccoon had the loveliest ears and he looked at his own ears and was sadder.

So it went—as Rabbit went from home to home he got sadder and sadder—comparing his features with those of the other animals.

The fact that the other animals thought Rabbit looked just fine didn't matter to him. Finally, Rabbit decided he was going to do something about "his problem"—that he was going to go to the Feast in a lovely new coat.

Of all of the animals, the prettiest coat is probably Otter's. So Rabbit decided he was going to wear Otter's coat to the Feast. He made his PLANS.

Now in the old days, Otter was a little different from today. In those days, Otter was a mountain animal and lived way up on the side of the hill rather than down by the river like today. The path to his house went from way up the side of the hill, down to the River, where it joined the path to the village. On the day of the Feast, Rabbit made his plans and built a fire right where the path from Otter's house met the river. Next to fire he put a big shovel. He sat down on a log and waited for Otter to come.

Just a little before sunset, Otter came down the hill.

"Rabbit, aren't you going to the Feast?"

Rabbit replied "Yes, but first I'm going to sit here and watch the stars fall from the sky".

"Watch the stars fall from the sky? What do you mean?" Otter asked.

Rabbit said "Well on certain very special nights—and this is one of those nights—at certain very special places—and this is one of those special places- if you sit quietly after sunset, you can see the stars fall from the sky. It is very beautiful. Would you like to join me?"

Well, Otter had never seen this before so he sat down on a log and as soon as he did, Rabbit put another log on the fire—and another—and another—until he had a really big fire going. Otter started to be uncomfortable from the heat. "Awful warm this evening, don't you think Rabbit?"

Rabbit replied--"Why don't you take your coat off and hang it from this tree? You'll feel cooler without it".

Sure enough Otter was much more comfortable without his coat and he sat there and slowly got sleepy—the way you do around a fire.

Just about the time that Otter was nearly asleep, Rabbit jumped up and pointed to the West and said "Look Otter, the stars are starting to fall". As soon as Otter looked West, Rabbit reached into the fire with the shovel he had there and threw some burning coals up in the air.

"Otter—Look OUT the stars are falling too close! Quick, jump in the river!"

As soon as Otter jumped in the river, Rabbit took Otter's coat, put it on and went to the Feast.

Well, it didn't take long for Chief Bear to notice that something was wrong because there in the Dance Circle was Rabbit wearing Otter's coat. Same long ears, same fluffy tail but Otter's coat.

"Rabbit—Why are you wearing Otter's coat?"

Rabbit pointed to the coat and said "Look, NO, I'm Otter—See?"

Chief Bear asked again "Rabbit—Why are you wearing Otter's coat?"

Rabbit again pointed to the coat and said "Look, NO, I'm Otter—See??"

Well, Chief Bear took one claw and reached over and split Rabbit's nose in two.

"Rabbit—Take Otter back his coat". Rabbit looked down and said, "Yes sir" and went back to where he had left Otter.

Rabbit shouted out into the water "Otter, Chief Bear says you're late for the Feast. He wants you there now!" And Rabbit helped Otter on with his coat.

Two things are true to this day. One is that Creator left Rabbit with a split in his nose to remind him not to play tricks on the other animals. The other is that Otter so enjoyed his swim in the river that he moved down from the mountain and lives by the river today.

That is what the old people tell us.

# The Boy and The Rattlesnake
## retold by
## Gray Owl

Several tribes have versions of this story—this is the one I heard as a child - Gray Owl

In many different tribes, the time comes when a boy becomes a man by doing a Vision Quest. (Girls have their own ceremonies but, since I am a man, I don't know about them).

The boy will take his knife and maybe a blanket and head out alone without food onto the prairie or into the forest or up a mountain. He will be alone for days, praying to Creator to give him a vision and to tell him what Creator wants him to do with his life.

It was now time for one young man to go forth to become a man. He asked his grandfather what he should do. The grandfather, being a wise man and knowing that the journey and the praying was what was important said, "On the top of that mountain is one tree that is taller than all the others. At the top of that tree is one leaf that if different from the others. Go and find that leaf—Go and find Creator's will for your life".

So the boy set out and pretty soon was climbing the mountain. The climbing got harder and harder and by the second day he was using hands and feet to climb places where he could not stand up.

When he was almost to the top of the mountain he heard a voice shouting, "Help me! Help me! I've fallen into a hole and I can't climb out!" So the boy shouted back and by following the sound of the voice, eventually found himself standing at the top of a large hole in the ground. But when he looked down into the hole, all he saw was a rattlesnake at the bottom. "Are you the one who was calling to me?" he asked.

The snake reared up and said, "Yes, I can't get out. Help me!" "Climb down in the hole and help me get out".

"Climb down in the hole with a rattlesnake? NO WAY!" and the boy started to walk away. The snake continued to call out "Help me! Help me!"

The boy had only gotten a short distance when he started to wonder. "Is this what I am supposed to do? Is this Creator's way of speaking to me?"

So the boy went back to the top of the hole and called down to the snake "If I come down there will you promise not to bite me? If you bite me I will surely die!"

The snake said, "Why should I bite you? You will be helping me".

So the boy climbed down the hole—which was deeper than he thought—and tried to help the snake get out but the hole was too deep.

The snake said- "If you hang me around your neck you can use both hands to climb".

To which the boy said "Hang you around my neck? You'll bite me and I will die".

But the rattlesnake reassured him by saying "You will be helping me, I have no reason to bite you".

So the boy looped the snake around his neck and climbed to the top. Putting the snake down carefully he said "Goodbye. I have to get back to my vision quest now".

But the snake said, "No, you have to help me get back down the mountain side. It's starting to get very cold!  If you leave me up here I will freeze. I shall surely die".

Finally, the boy agreed and started to carry the snake down the mountain—sometimes in his hands and sometimes looped around his neck.

The snake started to complain, "I'm so cold. I'm freezing to death. Put me inside your shirt and I will be warm".

"Put you inside my shirt—no way! If you bite me I'll die".

But again the snake reassured him, "You are helping to save my life, why would I bite you?"

So the boy took his belt and made a big pouch out of his shirt and continued to carry the snake down the mountain.

Just at the point where the mountain became a gentle hill, the boy felt a terrible pain in his side and when he pulled out his shirt he saw the snake's fangs buried in his stomach.

He threw the snake down and said, "You promised you wouldn't bite me! Now I'm going to die!"

As the snake slithered away he turned back and said, "Don't blame me! You only have yourself to blame. You knew what I was when you picked me up!"

This story is told to children at a young age and later—maybe when they become teenagers and have friends their parents aren't happy about, they will be told the story again and reminded "You knew what he was when you picked him up".

# The Maid of the Mist
## (Ongiaras)
### retold by
### Hawkwoman

She lost her husband and her hope at a young age, and the beautiful girl could not find her way through the sorrow upon sorrow that was her lot in life. So she stepped one day into her canoe, singing a death song softly to herself, and paddled out into the current. Soon the canoe was caught by the rough waves and hurtled toward the falls. But as it pitched over and she fell, Heno, the god of thunder who lived in the falls, caught the maiden gently in his arms and carried her to his home beneath the thundering veil of water.

Heno and his sons ministered to the grieving girl, and she stayed with them until her heart healed within her. Then the younger son spoke words of love to the maiden and they married, to the delight of the god of thunder. A young son was born to the couple, and he followed his grandfather everywhere, learning what it meant to be a god of thunder.

The only shadow on the happiness of the maiden in the mist was a continual longing to see her people one more time. Her chance came in an unexpected and unwelcome way. A great snake came down the mighty river and poisoned the waters of her people. They grew sick and were dying. Soon the snake would return to devour the dead until the people were all gone. It was Heno himself who gave her the news, and she begged that she might return for one hour to warn her people of the danger. The god himself lifted her through the falls and set her down among her people to give warning about the evil snake that was causing such pestilence among them. She advised them to move to a higher country until the danger was past, and they agreed. Then Heno came and took the maiden back to her husband and her home.

In a few days, the giant serpent returned to the village, seeking the bodies of those who had died from the poison it had spread. When the snake realized that the people had deserted the village, it hissed in rage and turned upstream to search for them. But Heno heard the voice of the serpent and rose up through the mist of the falls. He threw a great thunderbolt at the creature and killed it in one mighty blast. The giant body of the creature floated downstream and lodged just above the cataract, creating a large semi-circle that deflected huge amounts of water into the falls at the place just above the god's home. Horrified by this disastrous turn of events, Heno swept in through the falls and did his best to stop the massive influx of water, but it was too late.

Seeing that his home would soon be destroyed, Heno called for the maiden and his sons to come away with him. The younger son caught up his wife and child and followed Heno through the water of the falls and up into the sky, where the Thunderer made them a new home. From this place, they watch over the people of the earth, while Heno thunders in the clouds as he once thundered in the vapors of the great falls. To this day, an echo of the Heno's voice can be heard in the thunder of the mighty waters of Niagara Falls.

That is what the old people tell us.

## Why the Bat Flies Alone
### retold by
### Gray Owl

A long time ago, the old people tell, the world was a very different place. Before the human beings came, all of the animals lived together in towns and villages much like the people do today. One day the Eagle, who was the Chief of all of the Birds decided to have a great feast and invited all of the birds to come and celebrate the fine weather and the good season they had had. About two days before the feast, Tlomeha the Bat came to him and asked, "Why haven't I been invited to the feast with the other birds?" The Eagle pulled back and said "But you are not a bird".  But Tlomeha looked at him and said, "It is true that I don't have feathers but I can fly as well as any of you—and better than most. Who says I am not a bird?"

This caused the Eagle to think long and hard and he realized that the differences between the Bat and himself were no greater than the differences between the sparrow and the owl. Because Eagle was a great leader and had a great heart, he knew that he had been wrong. "Please, come to feast and you shall be our guest of honor to make up for not having invited you in the first place". Tlomeha agreed and sat next to the Eagle at the feast. All of the birds were there each in his kind but as Tlomeha looked around he saw that Vulture was sitting all alone outside the Circle. He asked the Eagle why this was so and the Eagle responded that the vulture smelled from the carrion he ate and wouldn't clean up even for a feast and so they made him sit alone so they could enjoy their meal. Bat thought about this briefly but soon was engaged in conversation on other things. Bat had a wonderful meal and was honored greatly by the Birds with gifts and many praises.

A few days later, Bear-who was the Chief of the Animals-heard about the feast the Birds had had and decided this was a really good idea so he scheduled a feast of his own. About two days before the feast, Tlomeha the Bat came to him and asked, "Why haven't I been invited to the feast of the Animals?" And Bear sat back and said "But you fly".  Bat was quick to point out that he and his kind had live young and that was- in fact – a cousin to the Mouse and the Rats and while it was true that he flew, so did the Flying Squirrel and HE had been invited. Chief Bear thought for the briefest time, and because he was a wise and honest leader he admitted that he had been wrong and invited Tlomeha to be the

Guest of Honor at the Feast and to sit next to him in the Center of the Circle.

On the night of the feast Tlomeha watched all of the animals. Chief Bear was smart enough to have the hunters and the grazers in separate parts of the Circle but everyone was there. As he looked around at all of the animals, he noticed that one animal, the Skunk, was sitting alone. When he asked Chief Bear about this, Bear responded that Skunk was mean-tempered and smelled bad and tended to spray people with his foul scent and so he was made to eat apart. Tlomeha had a great time and was honored by speeches and gifts the other animals had brought to make up for the slight of not inviting him.

A few days later, it chanced that Chief Bear and Chief Eagle met for business and began to discuss their feasts. "We had a great feast"—proclaimed the Eagle. "We even had Tlomeha the Bat as our Guest of Honor." "What?" shouted Chief Bear- "He was the Guest of Honor at out feast as well!" It didn't take long for the two Chiefs to figure out how they had been had and they immediately sent for Tlomeha to explain why he had done what he had done. But Tlomeha was a coward and he slunk away rather than face the Chiefs. To this day—Tlomeha the Bat only flies at night and avoids the other animals and birds who know how dishonorable he is. Not even the Vulture or Skunk will have anything to do with him.

This is what the old people tell us.

Heron and the Hummingbird
(Hitchiti Tribe)
retold by
Hawkwoman

Heron and Hummingbird were very good friends, even though one was tall and gangly and awkward and one was small and sleek and fast. They both loved to eat fish. The Hummingbird preferred small fish like minnows and Heron liked the large ones.

One day, Hummingbird said to his friend: "I am sure there are enough fish in the world for both of our kind to eat. Why don't we have a race to see which of us should own the fish?"

Heron thought that was a very good idea. They decided that they would race for four days. The finish line was an old dead tree next to a far-away river. Whichever of them sat on top of the tree first on the fourth day of the race would own all the fish in the world.

They started out the next morning. The Hummingbird zipped along, flying around and around the Heron, who was moving steadily forward, flapping his giant wings. Then the pretty flowers along the way would distract Hummingbird. He would flit from one to the other, tasting the nectar. When Hummingbird noticed that Heron was ahead of him, he hurried to catch up with him, zooming ahead as fast as he could, and leaving Heron far behind. Heron just kept flying steadily forward, flapping his giant wings.

Hummingbird was tired from all his flitting. When it got dark, he decided to rest. He found a nice spot to perch and slept all night long. But Heron just kept flying steadily forward, flapping his giant wings.

For two more days, the Hummingbird and the Heron raced toward the far-distant riverbank with the dead tree that was the finish line. Hummingbird had a marvelous time sipping nectar and flitting among the flowers and resting himself at night. Heron stoically kept up a steady flap-flap-flapping of his giant wings, propelling himself forward through the air all day and all night.

Hummingbird woke from his sleep the morning of the fourth day, refreshed and invigorated. He flew zip-zip toward the riverbank with its dead tree. When it came into view, he saw Heron perched at the top of the tree! Heron had won the race by flying straight and steady through the night while Hummingbird slept.

So from that day forward, the Heron has owned all the fish in the rivers and lakes, and the Hummingbird has sipped from the nectar of the many flowers which he enjoyed so much during the race.

That is what the old people tell us.

Why the Badger is the way he is
retold by
Gray Owl
I was told this story as a child but I have never seen it in print.

A long time ago, the old people tell us, the animals and the people lived much closer together than they do today. There was at that time a "person" who today would be called a skin-walker or a shape shifter or a Raven-Mocker or witch or a wizard. He had many "Tricks" that he would carry in his medicine bag and he could do many things. He was very old and the truth is that he had changed shapes so many times that he no longer remembered whether he had originally been born as a human or as an animal or even what kind of animal it might have been. Over the many years of his life, he had lived in caves, in cabins, in tipis, in hogans and in grass huts-- once he had even lived in a large city many miles to the south.

He did not consider himself evil but he admitted that if he wanted something he would just take it and that some would consider him a thief. It always happened that eventually those living around him would suspect the truth and eventually he would be forced to move on. The animals were always the first to figure it out and when he went out on his hunts, all the males of the flock, or the pack or the herd would join together against him. It always took the humans longer to figure it out and he could stay longer with them but eventually the humans would figure out something was wrong and they would start to watch him more closely. This didn't bother him much because among his medicines he had the power to make himself "unseen". He would reach into his medicine bag and take the proper plants and such and walk unseen right past the warriors--and when he got into the woods he would laugh at them.

But one evening, he heard noises outside the cabin and looked through the chinks in the wood to see that the cabin was surrounded by warriors. His first thought was to use his medicine to make himself unseen but he saw that the men had prepared for that and had smoky fires burning with wet cattails to make lots of smoke and that they would certainly see his form in the smoke. He then thought that perhaps he should change himself into a lion or a bear or maybe a fast stag and try to force his way past the men. But the sight of all of the bows and lances told him that he would not get ten feet before he would be full of holes. He then looked up at the smoke hole in the cabin ceiling and thought of becoming a bird-- until he remembered that this tribe was famous for their ability to shoot down birds with their arrows.

Looking around, he decided that his only way of escape was to tunnel out through the dirt floor and so he reached into his medicine bag and took out the medicines to make himself into several different animals at once. He decided he needed long sharp claws to dig and sharp teeth in case he had to chew through roots—and he needed very strong arms to push away the dirt and any rocks he encountered. When he was done he didn't look like any other animal but he was perfect for digging. So he set to work and quickly dug himself out of the cabin and all the way to the edge of the woods. When he dug himself out from under a tree he ran deeper into the forest to get away from the humans—and he started to laugh. Soon, however, his laughter turned to shrieks of rage because he realized that somewhere along the way he had lost his medicine bag and that he couldn't make the medicines to change his form again with his hands the way they are. Later, when the humans saw him, they didn't recognize his animal form and they named him Badger.

Some tribes honor the Badger because they say he is so fierce but the truth is that he is not brave and what people see as fierce is really his anger at being trapped in that form and, in truth, he is just bad tempered.

This is what the old people tell us.

Rainbow Crow<br>(Lenni Lenape Tribe)<br>retold by<br>Hawkwoman

It was so cold. Snow fell constantly, and ice formed over all the waters. The animals had never seen snow before. At first, it was a novelty, something to play in. But the cold increased tenfold, and they began to worry. The little animals were being buried in the snowdrifts and the larger animals could hardly walk because the snow was so deep. Soon, all would perish if something were not done.

"We must send a messenger to Creator" said Wise Owl. "We must ask him to think the world warm again so that Spirit of the Snow will leave us in peace."

The animals were pleased with this plan. They began to debate among themselves, trying to decide whom to send up to the Creator. Wise Owl could not see well during the daylight, so he could not go. Coyote was easily distracted and like playing tricks, so he could not be trusted. Turtle was steady and stable, but he crawled too slowly. Finally, Rainbow Crow, the most beautiful of all the birds with shimmering feathers of rainbow hues and an enchanting singing voice, was chosen to go to the Creator.

It was an arduous journey, three days up and up into the heavens, past the trees and clouds, beyond the sun and the moon, and even above all the stars. He was buffeted by winds and had no place to rest, but he carried bravely on until he reached Heaven. When Rainbow Crow reached the Holy Place, he called out to the Creator, but received no answer. The Creator was too busy thinking up what would be to notice even the most beautiful of birds. So Rainbow Crow began to sing his most beautiful song.

The Creator was drawn from his thoughts by the lovely sound, and came to see which bird was making it. He greeted Rainbow Crow kindly and asked what gift he could give the noble bird in exchange for his song. Rainbow Crow asked the Creator to un-think the snow, so that the animals of Earth would not be buried and freeze to death. But the Creator told Rainbow Crow that the snow and the ice had spirits of their own and could not be destroyed.

"What shall we do then?" asked the Rainbow Crow, "We will all freeze or smother under the snow."

"You will not freeze," the Creator reassured him, "For I will think of Fire, something that will warm all creatures during the cold times."

The Creator stuck a stick into the blazing hot sun. The end blazed with a bright glowing fire, which burned brightly and gave off heat. "This is Fire," he told Rainbow Crow, handing him the cool end of the stick. "You must hurry to Earth as fast as you can fly before the stick burns up."

Rainbow Crow nodded his thanks to the Creator and flew as fast as he could go. It was a three-day trip to Heaven, and he was worried that the Fire would burn out before he reached the Earth. The stick was large and heavy, but the fire kept Rainbow Crow warm as he descended from Heaven down to the bright path of the stars. Then the Fire grew hot as it came closer to Rainbow Crows feathers. As he flew past the Sun, his tail caught on fire turning the shimmering beautiful feathers black. By the time he flew passed the moon, his whole body was black with soot from the hot Fire. When he plunged into the Sky and flew through the clouds, the smoke got into his throat, strangling his beautiful singing voice.

By the time Rainbow Crow landed among the freezing-cold animals of Earth, he was black as tar and could only Caw instead of sing. He delivered the fire to the animals, and they melted the snow and warmed themselves, rescuing the littlest animals from the snowdrifts where they lay buried.

It was a time of rejoicing, for Tindeh – Fire – had come to Earth. But Rainbow Crow sat apart, saddened by his dull, ugly feathers and his rasping voice. Then he felt the touch of wind on his face. He looked up and saw Creator walking towards him.

"Do not be sad, Rainbow Crow," the Creator said, "All animals will honor you for the sacrifice you made for them. And when the people come, they will not hunt you, for I have made your flesh taste of smoke so that it is no good to eat and your black feathers and hoarse voice will prevent man from putting you into a cage to sing for him. You will be free."

Then the Creator pointed to Rainbow Crow's black feathers. Before his eyes, Rainbow Crow saw the dull feathers become shiny and inside each one, he could see all of the colors of the rainbow. "This will remind everyone who sees you of the service you have been to your people," he said," and the sacrifice you made that saved them all."

And so shall it ever be.

That is what the old people tell us.

How the Red Bird Got His Color
(Cherokee)
retold by
Hawkwoman

Raccoon (Gv li) loved to tease Wolf (wa ya).  One day, Raccoon teased Wolf so much that Wolf became very angry and began to chase Raccoon through the woods. Raccoon, being the clever animal that he is, kept ahead of Wolf.

Raccoon came to a river but instead of jumping in the river, he quickly climbed a tall tree and peered over a branch to see what Wolf would do next.

When Wolf came to the river, he saw Raccoon's reflection in the water. Thinking that it was Raccoon, the Wolf jumped in and tried to catch him. Wolf continued to search for Raccoon for such a long time that he became so tired he nearly drowned. Finally, tired and exhausted, he climbed up the riverbank and fell fast asleep. After a while, Raccoon quietly climbed down the tree and slipped over to the sleeping wolf. While Wolf slept, Raccoon began to plaster the wolf's eyes with mud. Then when he had finished, Raccoon ran off through the woods laughing to himself thinking of the clever trick he had played.

Later, Wolf woke up. He began to whine, "Oh, someone please help me. I can't see. I can't open my eyes." But no one came to help him.

At long last, Brown Bird heard the wolf's cries. He flew over to Wolf and landed on his shoulder. He said, "What's the matter Brother Wolf? Can I help you"? Wolf cried, "I can't open my eyes. Oh, please help me to see again." The Bird said, "I'm just a little brown bird but I will help you if I can." Wolf said, "Bird, if you can help me to see again, I will take you to a magic rock that oozes red paint. We will paint your feathers bright red.

Brown Bird began pecking away at the dried mud on Wolf's eyes. Soon Wolf could open his eyes again. True to his promise Wolf said, "Thank you, my brother, now jump up onto my shoulder." Away they ran through the woods to the rock that oozed red paint.

When they came to the rock, Wolf reached up and plucked a twig from a tree branch. He chewed the end of the twig until it was soft and pliable like the end of a paintbrush. Then he dipped the end of the twig into the red paint and began to paint the bird's feathers red.

When all of his feathers were red, Bird flew off to show his family and friend how beautiful he was. That is why, from that day to this, you can see Red Bird flying around the woods in Cherokee country.

That is what the old people tell us.

The Legend of the Cedar Tree
(Cherokee)
retold by
Hawkwoman

A long time ago when the Cherokee people were new upon the earth, they thought that life would be much better if there was never any night. They beseeched the Creator that it might be day all the time and that there would be no darkness.

The Creator heard their voices and made the night cease and it was day all the time. Soon, the forest was thick with heavy growth. It became difficult to walk and to find the path. The people toiled in the gardens many long hours trying to keep the weeds pulled from among the corn and other food plants. It got hot, very hot, and continued that way day after long day. The people began to find it difficult to sleep and became short tempered and argued among themselves.

Not many days had passed before the people realized they had made a mistake and, once again, they beseeched the Creator. "Please," they said, "we have made a mistake in asking that it be day all the time. Now we think that it should be night all the time." The Creator paused at this new request and thought that perhaps the people may be right even though all things were created in twos--- representing to us day and night, life and death, good and evil, times of plenty and those times of famine. The Creator loved the people and decided to make it night all the time as they had asked.

The day ceased and night fell upon the earth. Soon, the crops stopped growing and it became very cold. The people spent much of their time gathering wood for the fires. They could not see to hunt meat and with no crops growing it was not long before the people were cold, weak, and very hungry. Many of the people died.

Those that remained still living gathered once again to beseech the Creator. "Help us Creator," they cried! "We have made a terrible mistake. You had made the day and the night perfect, and as it should be, from the beginning. We ask that you forgive us and make the day and night as it was before."

Once again the Creator listened to the request of the people. The day and the night became, as the people had asked, as it had been in the beginning. Each day was divided between light and darkness. The weather became more pleasant, and the crops began to grow again. Game was plentiful and the hunting was good. The people had plenty to eat and there was not much sickness. The people treated each other with compassion and respect. It was good to be alive. The people thanked the Creator for their life and for the food they had to eat.

The Creator accepted the gratitude of the people and was glad to see them smiling again. However, during the time of the long days of night, many of the people had died, and Creator was sorry that they had perished because of the night. The Creator placed their spirits in a newly created tree. This tree was named a-tsi-na tlu-gv CEDAR TREE.

When you smell the aroma of the cedar tree or gaze upon it standing in the forest, remember that if you are Tsalagi (Cherokee), you are looking upon your ancestor.

That is what the old people tell us.

The Legend of the Cherokee Rose

(Cherokee)

retold by

Hawkwoman

In the latter half of 1838, Cherokee People who had not voluntarily moved west earlier were forced to leave their homes in the East.

The trail to the West was long and treacherous and many were dying along the way. The People's hearts were heavy with sadness and their tears mingled with the dust of the trail.

The Elders knew that the survival of the children depended upon the strength of the women. One evening around the campfire, the Elders called upon Heaven Dweller, (In Cherokee- ga lv la di e hi).. They told Him of the People's suffering and tears. They were afraid the children would not survive to rebuild the Cherokee Nation.

Gal v la di e hi spoke to them, "To let you know how much I care, I will give you a sign. In the morning, tell the women to look back along the trail. Where their tears have fallen, I will cause to grow a plant that will have seven leaves for the seven clans of the Cherokee Nation.  Amidst the plant will be a delicate white rose with five petals. In the center of the blossom will be a pile of gold to remind the Cherokee of the white man's greed for the gold found on the Cherokee homeland. This plant will be sturdy and strong with stickers on all the stems. It will defy anything which tries to destroy it."

The next morning the Elders told the women to look back down the trail. A plant was growing fast and covering the trail where they had walked. As the women watched, blossoms formed and slowly opened. They forgot their sadness. Like the plant the women began to feel strong and beautiful. As the plant protected its blossoms, they knew they would have the courage and determination to protect their children who would begin a new Nation in the West.

The entire Nation did not go West. Some escaped North into Virginia (Now West Virginia) and other places to hide out in the Appalachian Mountains. Among these people were my People.

That is what the old people tell us.

Rabbit Teaches the Wolves to Dance<br>retold by<br>Gray Owl

One day, Rabbit was walking down the trail and walked into a clearing. He was almost at the center of the clearing when he noticed that he was surrounded by five Wolves.

"Good Morning Wolves. What are you doing?"

The leader of the Wolves smiled and said, "We're getting ready to have lunch"

"What are you having for lunch?"

The Wolf smiled and said "Rabbit."

Now Rabbit knew he had to think fast if he wanted to survive so he stepped back and said, "Well, you got me for sure and I won't fight. But it's too bad because I just came up with a new dance step and I haven't had a chance to teach it to anybody yet." Now Rabbit knew that he couldn't have said anything better because the only thing Wolves like more than singing is dancing.

The head Wolf thought for a second and said, "Well, you can teach it to us BEFORE we eat you."

So Rabbit made up an intricate dance step and showed it to the Wolves. "HMMM! That's interesting. Let's see it again."

So Rabbit stood next to the Head Wolf and started to teach him the step.

"That's almost right but we need a Drum beat." So Rabbit walked over to the nearest tree and started a Drum beat.-Drum, Drum, Drum, DRUM! Drum, Drum, Drum, DRUM!

"Now you're getting it! But I need a better Drum." So Rabbit walked from one tree to the next until he found a tree at the edge of the clearing that had a good sound and started his Drum beat.

"That's great. Now you other Wolves stand next to your Chief and see if you can do it."

Pretty soon Rabbit had all five wolves dancing in a line in the center of the clearing.

"That's great! Keep it up you stupid wolves" and Rabbit took off running as fast as he could, followed by five hungry wolves.

Now a scared Rabbit can run pretty fast but a hungry Wolf can run pretty fast too and the Wolves would have caught Rabbit if he hadn't seen a hollow tree up ahead.

Rabbit jumped into the hollow tree and scrunched down as small as he could get.

Pretty soon one of the wolves reached down into the tree trying to get to Rabbit.

Rabbit looked around and saw a bunch of old acorns, pinecones and such. He picked up a pinecone and threw it at the wolf's paw as hard as he could.

"I'm going to get you Rabbit!

 OUCH! OUCH! OUCH!"

Every time a wolf paw would come into the hole, Rabbit would throw a pinecone or a nut or some-such.

Finally, the Wolves gave up and left. After a while, when Rabbit was sure the Wolves had left, Rabbit climbed carefully out of the hole and went on his way.

Two things are true to this day. Now, Rabbit looks carefully before he enters a clearing.

And you know, if you watch Wolves dancing in the moonlight, you will see them doing the dance step Rabbit taught them.

How Raccoon got her Striped Tail
(Traditional Cherokee Story)
retold by
Gray Owl

A long time ago, the old people tell us, the world was a very different place. In those days, raccoon didn't look like she does today but was brown from the tip of her nose to the tip of her tail. Just as today, raccoon was a little greedy and not above stealing what she wanted if she couldn't get it another way.

One evening when raccoon came out of her home she looked up and saw the first star of the evening and it was SO BEAUTIFUL that she wanted it desperately---and what she wanted, she always tried to get.

She reached out as high as she could but she couldn't quite reach the star. She tried standing on a nearby stump but she still couldn't reach the star. So she decided that she needed to climb the highest tree in the forest and SURELY, she would be able to catch that star. She knew just which tree she needed to climb and she started out for it but when she reached the tree she found that Yona the BEAR was sitting under the tree guarding it.

Yona inquired---quite politely actually – what raccoon was doing there and when she told him that she was going to climb the tree he told her in no uncertain terms that this was HIS tree and there was a hive of bees near the top—and that he was just waiting for them to fill the hive with honey and that he didn't want anybody disturbing his meal.

Raccoon took one more step closer to the tree but Bear's growls persuaded her that she wasn't going to climb that tree with Bear guarding it so well.

Raccoon went down to the stream to think. She so wanted that star. Maybe, she thought, she could quietly sneak around to the other side of the tree and climb where Bear couldn't see her. Just to make sure she wasn't seen, she reached down into the stream and took a little bit of the black mud and made a mask over her eyes---just in case Bear saw her.

She went to the other side of the tree and crept ever so silently up to the tree and started to climb---Oh so carefully so as to not let

Bear know what she was up to. Slowly, slowly up to the top. When she reached the very top she reached out to grab the star.

BUT JUST THEN---she felt a terrible pain in her tail and looked down to see that Bear was right below her with his strong paw and claws wrapped around her tail. She hadn't fooled Bear at all and he had climbed up right behind her one branch at a time.

She started to scream and things might have gotten bad but just then Creator decided to intervene—for he loved both Bear and Raccoon. Creator sent a burst of power down and suddenly Bear's claws glowed white-hot and he let go of her tail to blow on his paw. OF course, Raccoon scampered away as quickly as she could.

Several things remain unchanged from that day. Bear's claws are now always black. Raccoon still wears her mask and now her tail is permanently striped where Bear's claws held her.

But you know, Creator is always loving and if you look carefully into raccoon's eyes, you will see the sparkle of that star that she wanted so much.

This is what the old people tell us and we know it is true.


Raven and Crow's Giveaway
retold by
Gray Owl


The Potlatch or Giveaway is a custom of many Native American tribes. The Old People tell us that before the Human Beings came, it was also the custom of the animals.

One day, Raven was visiting his neighbor Crow when Crow mentioned that he had had a very good year and was going to have a Giveaway. Now Old Raven is a smart bird and he thought about how to turn this to HIS advantage.

"Say Crow, since I have a bigger home next door, why don't we do it at my house and I'll invite all of the Birds and Animals to come."

While Crow thought about this, Raven came up with a brilliant idea. "Crow, you have such a lovely voice. Why don't you greet all of the guests with a song? They will really love that."

Now, Crow didn't get a chance to sing before an audience all that often so he thought it was a great idea. He told Raven to go ahead and invite everyone and he would get together the food and gifts and practice his singing.

Of course, Raven invited everyone to his (Raven's)—not Crow's—Giveaway and he told everyone that Crow wanted to sing and that he (Raven) felt so sorry for Crow that he had agreed.

On the night of the Giveaway, Raven proceeded to give away Crow's food and gifts telling each Guest that they were his own gift.

Each time it looked like Crow was going to stop singing, Raven, would step up to him and flatter him saying---"Please don't stop. All of the animals are enjoying your singing so much!"

Of course, over the evening Crow's voice began to get tired and his voice got harsher and harsher until it was horrible to hear. All of the animals took their gifts and were gone before Crow finally stopped singing. Raven told him again how much each of the animals had loved his singing and how much it had added to the Giveaway.

That Winter and Spring, Raven was invited to all of the local Giveaways and always came away with nice gifts. Crow really didn't understand why he didn't get invited to more Giveaways but the truth is that everyone was afraid he would start singing again. But someday, Crow's voice will heal and he will again have a pleasant song.

Turtle and his Whistle
retold by
Gray Owl

A long time ago, Turtle had a whistle. It was a beautiful thing carved by Turtle's friend Beaver from very old wood from the bottom of the lake and it had wonderful tone. He would play his whistle for hours with the loveliest tunes and all of the animals would stop and listen at twilight. Today, no human being has ever heard a Turtle talk and no human being has ever heard a Turtle play the whistle and this is how that came to be.

One evening just at sunset Turtle was playing his whistle as he always did when Quail flew down to him. "Can I play on your lovely whistle, Turtle?" Quail asked oh-so-politely. "I want to see if I can learn and maybe have Beaver or Woodpecker make a whistle or flute for me."

Turtle thought about it for a minute and then agreed to let Quail try. After a few false notes, Quail began the prettiest song on the whistle. Turtle closed his eyes so that he could concentrate. He had played the whistle for so many years and now he was hearing it played by another animal. He liked the sound.

Quail walked around Turtle serenading him---from the side, from behind and from the other side. Pretty soon he knew that Turtle was almost asleep and took off and flew to the top of the highest tree. Of course Turtle was wide-awake instantly and he called to Quail to come back and bring back his whistle. Quail just made a rude noise and flew away. Turtle never got his whistle back and he's still so angry about it that he refuses to talk to anybody.

If he did talk, he would remind folks that sometimes the sweetest voices and the most reasonable sounding ideas might come from the biggest thieves and the darkest hearts.

THAT IS WHAT THE OLD PEOPLE TELL US.

# The Storytellers

**<u>Hawkwoman's Story</u>:**
My great-great-grandparents on my father's side were of Huron, Cherokee and Shawnee blood. They came up from Georgia and settled in Indian Valley, Floyd County, Virginia but my great-great grandmother was captured in a Huron village at Round Bottom, Virginia when she was a young girl. She said her mother ran into the woods and that was the last time she saw her.  The militia went to the village and caught her and took her to William Underwood, whose wife was Native American and was a Cherokee woman. William's mother was Shawnee and he owned a trading post at that time. His brother Joseph and Cherokee wife took her to raise and named her Mary (Polly). She later married William's son Joshua Underwood. They had to pay $150.00 to get a license to be married because she was "Indian".  Joshua and Polly had several children and moved to Peters Mountain to hide from the removal of the Native people to the West. Their child Eliza was my great-grandmother who died young and Joshua and Polly raised my grandmother until she married my grandfather in 1901.

My grandfather had Cherokee and Shawnee blood. My grandmother Omi told us of our Native heritage and made us promise not to tell anyone because she was afraid she would lose her land. She told us many stories and took my sister and I to the fields and woods to show us the plants to cure sickness. We would help her collect nuts for the winter and she never took a bag to collect them in but always used her long apron to carry them in. Grandmother Omi went with the local doctor to help with the sick. When the deadly flu hit our town our local Dr. Dunn and his family were all stricken. She went to their home and stayed to doctor them until they were well. Dr. Dunn's daughter told me later that she saved them all with her Indian medicine. I was very lucky to have a grandmother who wanted us to know our heritage. She has walked on but watches over me with love
Chief Virginia Hawkwoman Smith

Gray Owl's Story

My bloodlines are Cherokee and Irish on my Dad's side and Scots-Irish, Ojibwa and Mohawk on my Mother's side.  Among my earliest memories is living on an Air Force Base in Enlisted Family housing and listening to Mr. Starbuck—the Cherokee Grandfather who lived with the family next door—telling me the old traditional stories—some of which you will read here. Sitting and listening to Mr. Starbuck is possibly my second youngest memory. I loved the Cherokee stories of Rabbit and Possum and Otter and Bear and I loved to listen to the stories Mr. Starbuck told about his youth on the Reservation. We would sit on the wooden porch and dangle our feet in the sand and he would tell me so much and I loved him dearly because he treated me as "human being" and not just as a small child who was always underfoot the way most adults did.  I remember very clearly announcing to my mother one day when I was about 5 years old that I was going to be an Indian when I grew up and being delighted when she told me I already was one.

I hope that you will enjoy these stories as much as I did hearing them from Mr. Starbuck when I was 5 years old.

Wayne Gray Owl Appleton

Suzan A. M. McVicker

The Appalachian Mountains of West Virginia hold me in their embrace of kinship. As a child, I soaked in mountain imprints and set about painting and drawing those impressions. I developed an artist's indelible collection of memories of an enduring ridge shouldering the horizon in early morning fog; the freedom of a creek's oxbow through a snug valley meadow; and outdoor rooms of rhododendron sheltered by rock outcroppings.

Decades later, I learned how American Indian and Euro-American bloodlines run together through my veins. I could then see how my mound-building ancestors shaped places for their home towns in West Virginia mountain landscapes. Thousands of years after earthwork platforms were constructed, late spring snow with the smell of mud rising from under it still reveals a worn outline. The townhouse built on top of the platform was one of the gathering places where myths and legends of our Appalachian Native Ancestors were passed down through story, drama, and artwork. As a member of the Appalachian American Indians of West Virginia, when I design, draw, and paint scenes from traditional tribal stories, I feel the commission of our Ancestors to keep the lessons alive. With joy, I give the images that come to me to you who read the stories.

CPSIA information can be obtained
at www.ICGtesting.com
Printed in the USA
BVHW021135160122
626379BV00002B/19